For Janet and Neil

First published in 1989
Reprinted in this edition 1991
by Hutchinson Children's Books Ltd
An imprint of the Random Century Group Ltd
20 Vauxhall Bridge Road, London SW1V 2SA

Random Century Australia (Pty) Ltd
20 Alfred Street, Sydney, NSW 2016

Random Century New Zealand Ltd
PO Box 40-086, Glenfield, Auckland 10

Random Century South Africa (Pty) Ltd
PO Box 337, Bergvlei 2012, South Africa

Printed in Hong Kong

THE WINTER HEDGEHOG

Ann and Reg Cartwright

HUTCHINSON

London   Sydney   Auckland   Johannesburg

ONE COLD, MISTY AUTUMN AFTERNOON, THE hedgehogs gathered in a wood. They were searching the undergrowth for leaves for their nests, preparing for the long sleep of winter.

All that is, except one.

The smallest hedgehog had overheard two foxes talking about winter. 'What is winter?' he had asked his mother.

'Winter comes when we are asleep,' she had replied. 'It can be beautiful, but it can also be dangerous, cruel and very, very cold. It's not for the likes of us. Now go to sleep.'

But the smallest hedgehog couldn't sleep. As
evening fell he slipped away to look for winter.
When hedgehogs are determined they can move
very swiftly, and soon the little hedgehog was
far from home. An owl swooped down from
high in a tree.

  'Hurry home,' he called. 'It's time for your
long sleep.' But on and on went the smallest
hedgehog until the sky turned dark and the trees
were nothing but shadows.

The next morning, the hedgehog awoke to find
the countryside covered in fog. 'Who goes
there?' called a voice, and a large rabbit emerged
from the mist, amazed to see a hedgehog about
with winter coming on.

'I'm looking for winter,' replied the hedgehog.
'Can you tell me where it is?'

'Hurry home,' said the rabbit. 'Winter is on
its way and it's no time for hedgehogs.'

But the smallest hedgehog wouldn't listen.
He was determined to find winter.

Days passed. The little hedgehog found plenty of slugs and insects to eat, but he couldn't find winter anywhere.

Then one day the air turned icy cold. Birds flew home to their roosts and the animals hid in their burrows and warrens. The smallest hedgehog felt very lonely and afraid and wished he was asleep with the other hedgehogs. But it was too late to turn back now!

That night winter came. A frosty wind swept
through the grass and blew the last straggling
leaves from the trees. In the morning the whole
countryside was covered in a carpet of snow.

'Winter!' cried the smallest hedgehog. 'I've
found it at last.' And all the birds flew down
from the trees to join him.

The trees were completely bare and the snow sparkled on the grass. The little hedgehog went to the river to drink, but it was frozen. He shivered, shook his prickles and stepped on to the ice. His feet began to slide and the faster he scurried, the faster he sped across it. 'Winter is wonderful,' he cried. At first he did not see the fox, like a dark shadow, slinking towards him.

'Hello! Come and join me,' he called as the fox
reached the riverbank. But the fox only heard
the rumble of his empty belly. With one leap he
pounced on to the ice. When the little hedgehog
saw his sly yellow eyes he understood what the
fox was about. But every time he tried to run
away he slipped on the ice. He curled into a ball
and spiked his prickles.

   'Ouch!' cried the fox. The sharp prickles
stabbed his paws and he reeled towards the
centre of the river where he disappeared beneath
the thin ice.

   'That was close,' the smallest hedgehog cried
to himself. 'Winter is beautiful, but it is also
cruel, dangerous and very, very cold.'

Winter was everywhere: in the air, in the trees,
on the ground and in the hedgerows. Colder
and colder it grew until the snow froze under
the hedgehog's feet. Then the snow came again
and a cruel north wind picked it up and
whipped it into a blizzard. The night fell as black
as ink and he lost his way. 'Winter is dangerous
and cruel and very, very cold,' moaned the little
hedgehog.

   Luck saved him. A hare scurrying home gave
him shelter in his burrow. By morning the snow
was still falling, but gently now, covering
everything it touched in a soft white blanket.

The smallest hedgehog was enchanted as he watched the pattern his paws made. Reaching the top of a hill, he rolled into a ball and spun over and over, turning himself into a great white snowball as he went. Down and down he rolled until he reached the feet of two children building a snowman.

'Hey, look at this,' said the little girl; 'a perfect head for our snowman.'

'I'm a hedgehog,' he cried. But no one heard his tiny hedgehog voice.

The girl placed the hedgehog snowball on the snowman's body and the boy used a carrot for a nose and pebbles for the eyes. 'Let me out,' shouted the hedgehog. But the children just stood back and admired their work before going home for lunch.

When the children had gone, the cold and hungry hedgehog nibbled at the carrot nose. As he munched the sun came out and the snow began to melt. He blinked in the bright sunlight, tumbled down the snowman's body and was free.

Time went on. The hedgehog saw the world in its winter cloak. He saw bright red berries disappear from the hedgerows as the birds collected them for their winter larders. And he watched children speed down the hill on their sleighs.

The winter passed. One day the air grew warmer and the river began to flow again. A stoat, who had changed his coat to winter white, changed it back to brown. Then the little hedgehog found crocuses and snowdrops beneath the trees and he knew it was time to go home. Slowly he made his way back to the wood.

From out of every log, sleepy hedgehogs were emerging from their long sleep.

'Where have you been?' they called to the smallest hedgehog.

'I found winter,' he replied.

'And what was it like?' asked his mother.

'It was wonderful and beautiful, but it was also…'

'Dangerous, cruel and very, very cold,' finished his mother.

But she was answered by a yawn, a sigh and a snore and the smallest hedgehog was fast asleep.

THE PROUD AND
FEARLESS LION

For Molly Franklin

THE PROUD AND FEARLESS LION

Ann and Reg Cartwright

HUTCHINSON

London   Sydney   Auckland   Johannesburg

ONCE THERE WAS A PROUD AND FEARLESS LION. Every morning at the same time he would go into the jungle and roar his mighty roar. So terrifying was this roar that all the animals would run away and hide; and so loud was this roar that the ground would shake and the leaves would fall from the trees.

'That'll show 'em who's boss!' said the proud and fearless lion.

One night word went round the jungle that it would rain. 'There will be a great storm,' said the little mouse. 'We must all take shelter.'

The big animals sheltered in a cave, the smaller ones in holes in the ground, and the birds snuggled together in the trees.

'Pooh!' said the proud and fearless lion. 'A little rain never hurt anyone.' And just to show how proud and fearless he was, he climbed to the top of his favourite hill and went to sleep. All night long it rained and rained, but on he slept.

The next morning the rain had stopped and the jungle was unusually quiet. A gentle mist hung over the trees and everywhere was still. Mouse woke up, sniffed the air and listened for Lion's roar. But for the first time ever it did not come.

That's strange, thought Mouse.

One by one the animals emerged, and because there was no sign of Lion they were not afraid. Hippo decided to take a bath, but Mouse was curious to discover what had happened to Lion.

'I think we should go and search for him,' she squeaked.

'Whatever for?' grumbled Giraffe. 'He's always been a show-off, roaring and frightening us.'

'I know he makes a lot of noise,' said Mouse. 'But has he ever hurt you?'

The animals had to agree that Lion had never hurt anyone.

So the animals set off to look for Lion. They found him on top of his hill. He opened his mouth to roar, but only a little squeak came out, followed by ATISHOO! He was no longer a proud and fearless lion – just a soggy, saggy, snivelling lion with drooping whiskers.

'You don't look so frightening now,' said Mouse bravely. 'I think you have a bad attack of soricus throaticus. It's brought on by too much roaring and sleeping in the rain. We can cure you with honey and Eucalyptus leaves, but if we make you better you must promise not to frighten us again.'

Lion tried to say, 'I promise,' but he could only squeak and nod his head.

Mouse sent the bees off to search for
nectar to make into honey, and the animals
and birds collected the Eucalyptus leaves.
For two whole days they nursed and comforted
Lion; and for two whole nights he slept and
dreamed and sneezed and coughed. By the third
morning he began to feel better.

The proud and fearless lion stood up and stretched his legs. 'Good morning, animals,' he said politely. But there was no reply. He walked down his hill and into the jungle calling, 'Tiger! Hippo! Giraffe! Little Mouse! Is anybody there?'

But the jungle was as sad and silent as if the animals had never existed.

Lion searched through the jungle for many miles.
All of a sudden, the little mouse came scurrying
towards him.

'Oh, brave Lion,' she cried. 'Come quickly.
While you were sleeping two hunters came and
drove the animals into a cage. They are being
taken away from the jungle to join a circus.
Because I am so small, I managed to escape
through the bars.'

When Lion heard Mouse's story he began to feel his pride and fearlessness coming back. The jungle would not be the jungle without the animals. 'Climb on to my head, little one,' he said. 'We must go and find them.'

Mouse knew a short cut and Lion followed her directions through the deepest, darkest part of the jungle, where no flowers grew and only snakes lived under the tangled leaves.

On and on they went until they came to the very edge of the jungle. In the moonlight Lion and Mouse could see two hunters sitting by a camp fire. The poor animals were locked in a cage. It was a terrible sight! Elephant's trunk was all squashed up and Giraffe's neck was stuck between the bars.

That night Lion and Mouse lay down together and fell asleep trying to think of a plan to save the animals.

By the time the sun had risen over the jungle the next morning, they had a plan. Mouse sat on top of Lion's head so that only she could be seen over the top of the bush. 'Now squeak, Mouse,' whispered Lion. And Mouse squeaked as loudly as she could until the hunters heard her.

'That's the mouse who escaped!' shouted one hunter.

'After her!' called the other.

But that was their biggest mistake....

Lion leaped out from behind the bush, roaring the loudest and most terrifying roar he had ever roared. ROARRRRRRR! It echoed through the jungle, and the earth shook and the leaves fell from the trees.

'That'll show 'em!' said the proud and fearless lion.

The terrified hunters fell over, dropping their guns and the keys to the cage. Mouse picked up the keys and ran to free the animals.

Soon all the animals were out of the cage. 'Thank you, proud and fearless lion,' they said.

'No trouble,' Lion replied. 'Now let's teach those hunters a lesson!'

So they all lined up, the smallest on the left and the biggest on the right.

'Charge!' shouted Mouse. And the animals roared and chattered and squawked and screeched and they chased the hunters out of the jungle for ever.

As they trooped back home, Lion realized he had never felt quite so proud and fearless before. And he kept his promise never to frighten the animals again.

But if those hunters ever came back...well, that would be another story!

First published in 1989
Reprinted in this edition 1991
by Hutchinson Children's Books Ltd
An imprint of the Random Century Group Ltd
20 Vauxhall Bridge Road, London SW1V 2SA

Random Century Australia (Pty) Ltd
20 Alfred Street, Sydney, NSW 2016

Random Century New Zealand Ltd
PO Box 40-086, Glenfield, Auckland 10

Random Century South Africa (Pty) Ltd
PO Box 337, Bergvlei 2012, South Africa

Printed in Hong Kong

THE LAST
DODO

Ann and Reg Cartwright

HUTCHINSON

London   Sydney   Auckland   Johannesburg

K ING GLUT WAS A LARGE, FAT, GREEDY
    king who lived in a large damp,
    cold castle. Of all the things he liked
to eat, his favourite food was eggs.

   King Glut had a chef called Adrian.
Poor Adrian! His life was a misery. He
spent all day in the kitchen trying to
think of new recipes to please the king.
He served quail eggs, hens' eggs, duck
eggs, goose eggs, and even swan
eggs. He fried them, he scrambled
them, he curried them and he boiled
them; but the king was never satisfied.
'More! More!' he would cry. 'Can't you
try something different.'

One morning at breakfast, King Glut
read in his newspaper that a dodo's
egg had been spotted on a distant
island. 'A dodo's egg!' he cried, licking
his fat lips. 'What a delicacy. I must
have it.'

He ordered Adrian to prepare the
boat. 'There's no time to lose,' he cried.

When the boat was ready, King Glut climbed aboard, clutching a giant egg cup and spoon in readiness for the great event.

'Row harder, Adrian,' he shouted. 'We must be first to reach the egg.'

For three days and nights they crossed the ocean. One morning a great ship appeared on the horizon. It was the Green Dove.

'Ahoy there,' called the captain through his loud-hailer. 'Where are you bound with that egg cup? Not after the dodo's egg, I hope. It's the last one in the whole world and this ship is on a mission to protect it.'

'Oh, no, I'm not egg bound,' lied the king. 'And this? Why, it's no egg cup, it's my crown!' And he turned it upside down and put it on his head.

'Well, be careful,' warned the captain. 'There are rough seas ahead.'

But the king took no notice. He was determined to find the egg and nothing was going to stop him. He should have listened, though, for the sky suddenly turned dark. The sea became so rough, and the waves so high, that Adrian could not control the boat.

'Help!' he shouted, as a mighty wave, as high as a house, crashed over the little boat and turned it upside down. King Glut and Adrian gasped and spluttered and hiccupped and swallowed great mouthfuls of salty water as they were carried away.
Up on top of the wave they went and down the other side.

Just as they were losing hope of being saved they felt land beneath their feet. King Glut rubbed his eyes. 'An island,' he cried. 'We must be near the dodo's egg.'

But the island began to move....

It wasn't an island. It was an enormous whale!

A huge jet of water shot up into the air like a fountain. Then away the whale swam with King Glut and Adrian hanging on for dear life.

Even in this new danger, the king could not forget his greed. 'We'll *never* be the first now,' he spluttered, desperately hanging on to his cup and spoon.

For many hours the whale swam on. Then, through the mist, came a sound. Hoot! Hoot! Hoot! Hoot! It was the Green Dove coming to the rescue.

'There she blows,' shouted the captain, as he caught sight of the whale.

The captain hauled the wet and bedraggled pair on board. He kindly gave them supper and laid their soggy clothes out on deck to dry. Was the king grateful? Not a bit of it. He was congratulating himself on his good fortune. Now he would be *sure* to find the egg, with the good captain to guide him to it.

Next morning, as the mist began to clear, a small green island came into view. 'This is our destination,' said the captain. 'Here we will find the dodo's egg.'

'Not if I get to it first,' the king whispered to Adrian.

The captain moored his ship, and King Glut and Adrian followed him on to the beach. They found themselves in a beautiful bay surrounded by tall trees. 'Follow me,' said the captain, as he tiptoed into the undergrowth with King Glut and Adrian close behind.

Soon the captain stopped. He parted the leaves and there, nestled in the warm sand, was a magnificent egg. A dodo's egg. The very last one in the whole wide world.

King Glut pushed the captain aside. 'Mine! Mine!' he cried, grabbing the egg. 'Quick Adrian, boil some water. I'll have it poached!'

But then something happened. There was a rustle, and a crackle, and a pecking sound. A crack appeared in the egg, then another, and another. Out of the egg popped a baby dodo. 'Cheep!' it said, as it looked at the world for the first time.

'Ahh,' said the captain.

'Ahh, ahh,' said Adrian.

Then there was silence. Adrian and the captain watched as the dodo gave the king a sharp peck on the nose.

'Ahh, ahh, ahhhhh!' sighed the king.

He was enchanted. He dropped his egg cup and threw away his spoon. 'From this day on,' he declared, 'the eating of eggs will be banned throughout my whole kingdom.'

'And from this day on,' added the captain, 'the dodo will live in peace and safety on this unknown island.'

Then the Green Dove sailed for home. The king was true to his word. From that day to this he has never eaten another egg.

And the dodo? No one has ever found the island.
 Let's hope they never will!